Copyright © 2024 Laura Sigala
All rights reserved. No part of this
publication may be reproduced, distributed,
or transmitted in any form or by any means without
the prior written permission of the author.

Dedication

I would like to dedicate this book to:

- Coach Tammy M.S. Thank you for being my inspiration! You were an incredible P.E. Coach at our elementary school where we taught together.

Thank you.

Acknowledgment

Thank you to my family, Armando, James & Patty, and Steve & Lisa, for your love and support. Special thanks to Mr. Whitman, Mrs. Velasco, and my teacher friends Shannon, Colynne, Eva, Helena, Coach Tammy, and Dolores for your unwavering encouragement and support.

Look, it is Tammy and Tommy Tough! They are running very fast to the park. It is a nice and sunny day.

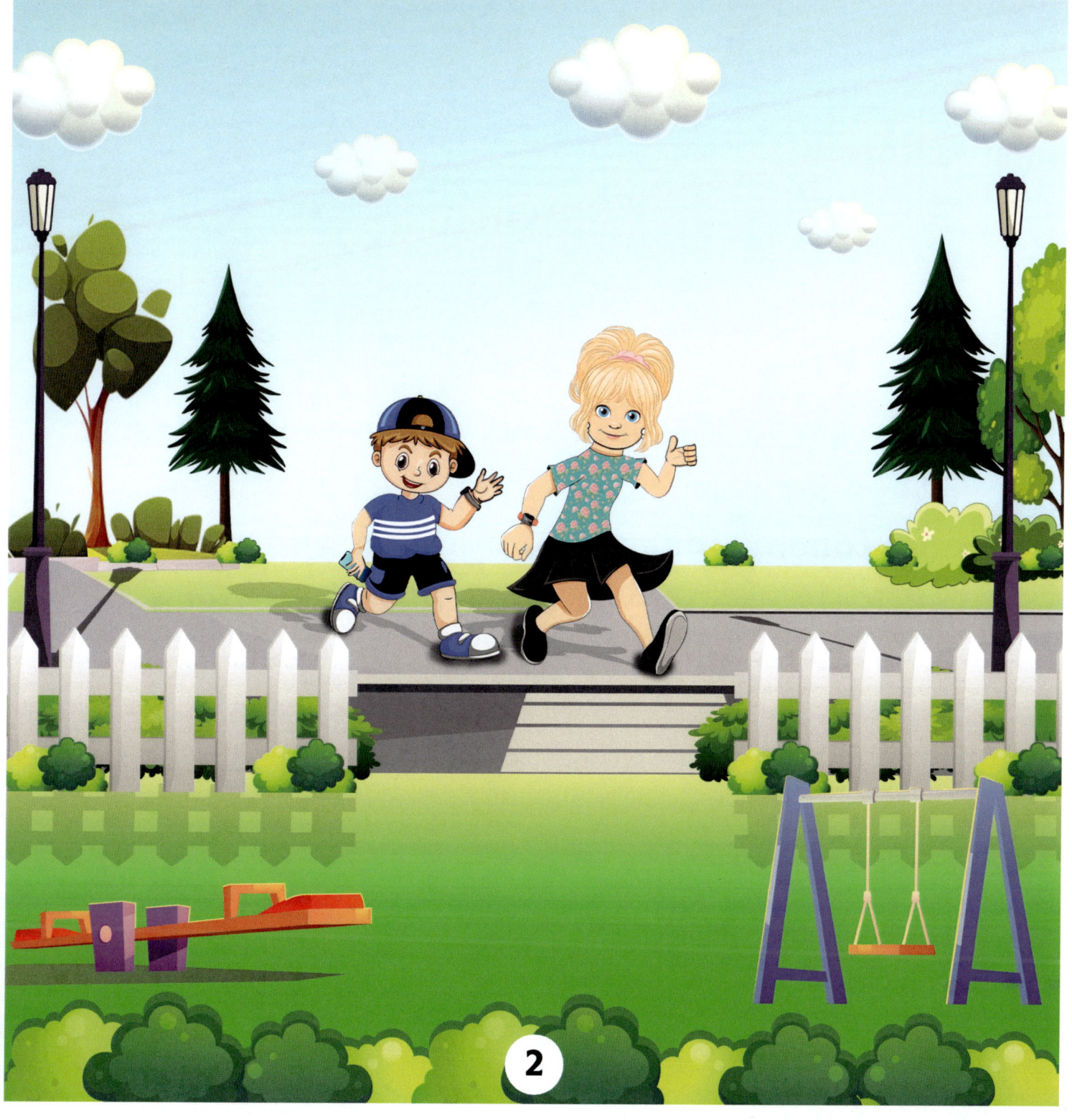

They get to the park and run to the swings. They jump on the swings quickly. Tammy and Tommy Tough swing higher and higher. It feels like they can touch the big green leaves on the very tall Oak trees.

Then, they decide to go to the slides that have a fort at the top. They run quickly to the slides. There are three slides to choose from. There's a very tall slide. There's a medium slide. Also, there is a small slide too.

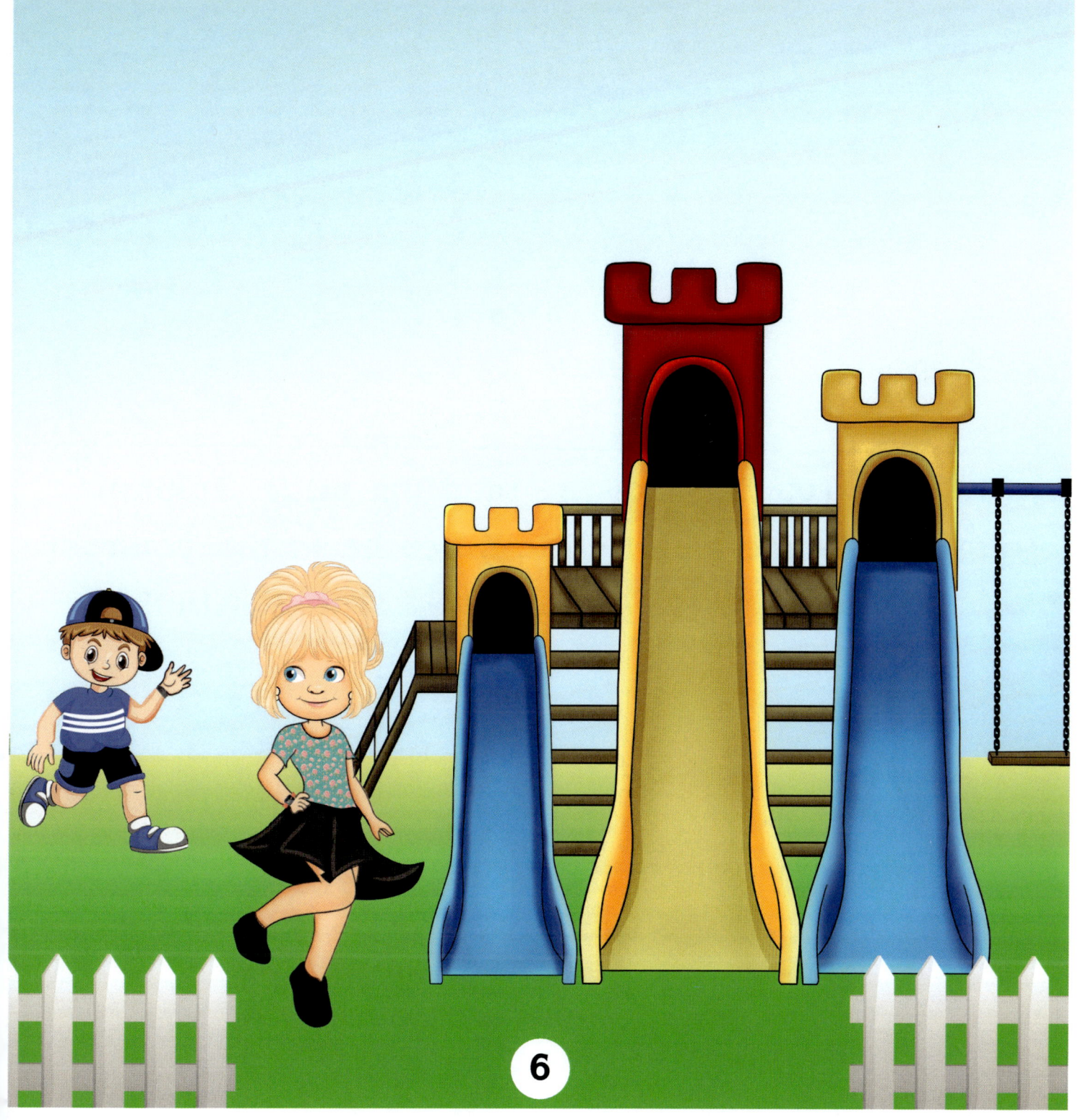

Tammy Tough picks the medium slide. Tommy Tough picks the small slide since he is the younger brother. The slides look like so much fun!

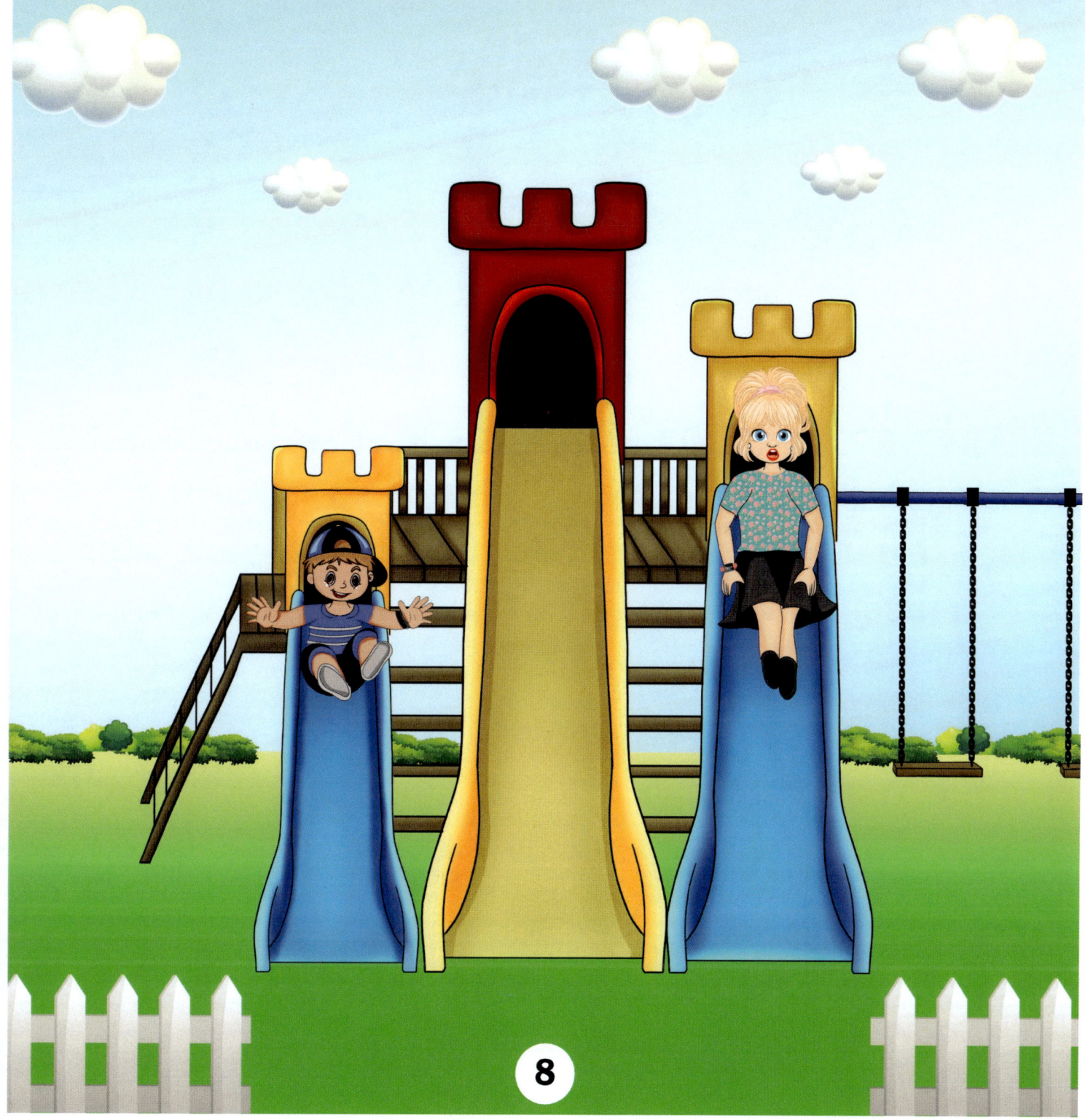

They go down the slides one at a time. Tammy Tough yells out, "Yipee! This is so much fun!" It's Tommy's turn next. Tommy Tough yells out, "Yipee! This is so much fun!" They ride down the slide several more times.

After going down the slides many times, Tammy and Tommy Tough decide to play on the fort. They walk over to the fort. Tammy looks at Tommy and says, "Do you want to play pirates now?" "Yes!" yelled Tommy.

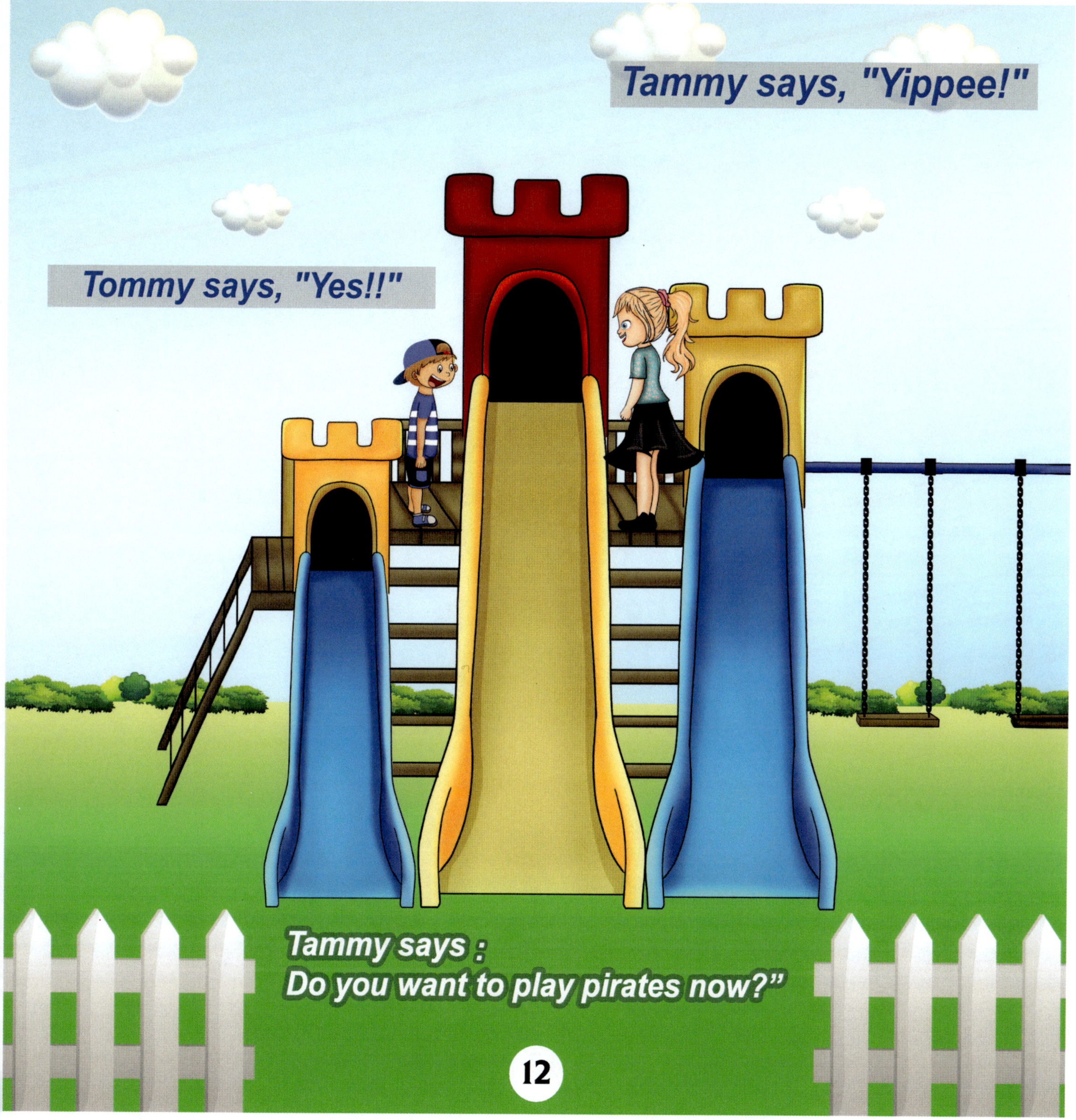

Tammy says, "Yippee!"

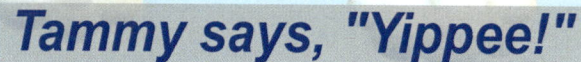

Tommy says, "Yes!!"

Tammy says :
Do you want to play pirates now?"

The kids take their swords out of the bag.
Tommy says, "Eye, eye matey!" to
Tammy. Tammy smiles back and laughs,
"Eye, eye matey!" to Tommy.
They both start to laugh
Ha! Ha! Ha! They play for a
long time together.

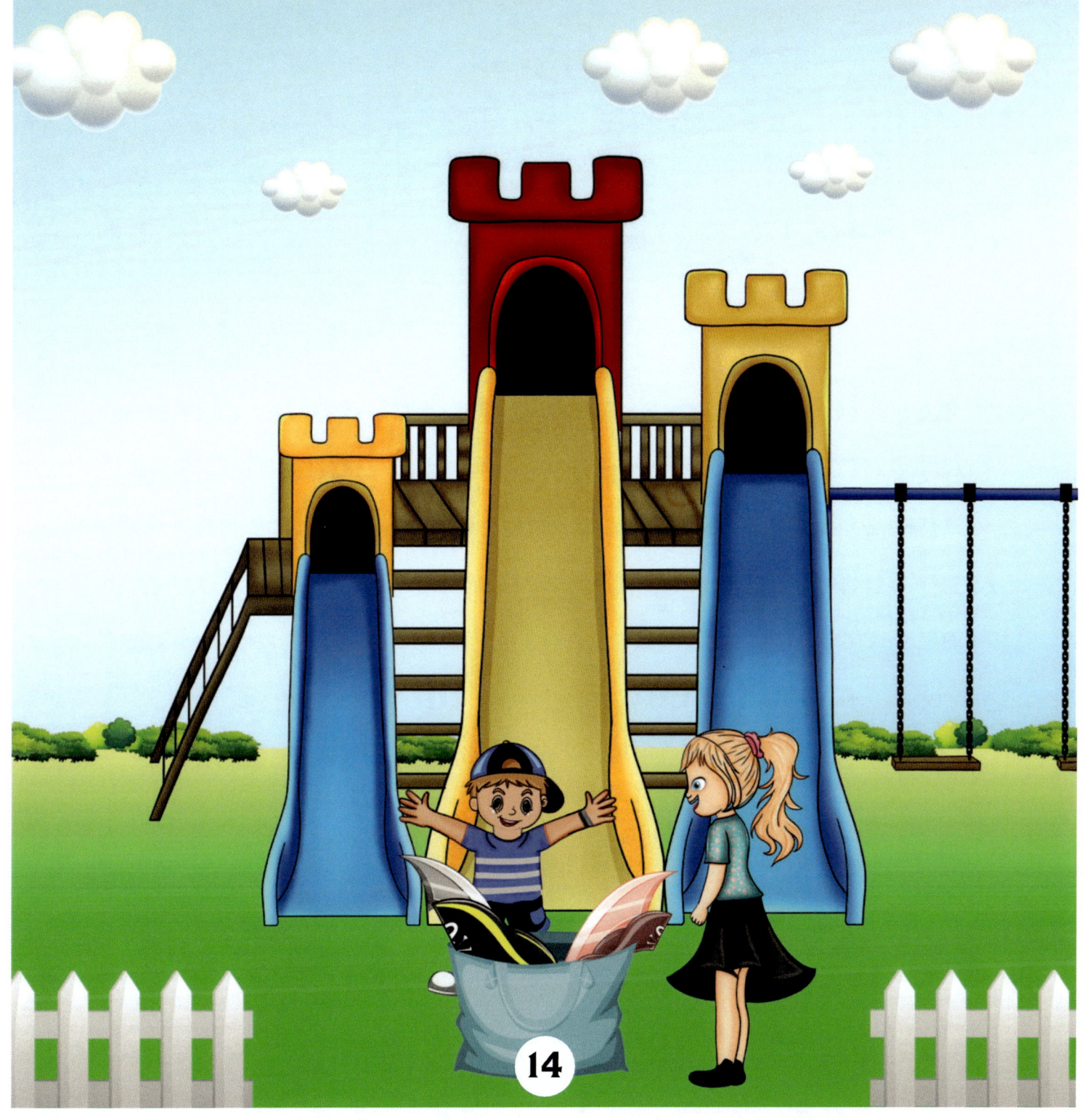

"Hey, let's have a sword fight!" yells Tammy Tough. "Unguard!' yells Tommy. "Cling! Clang!" the swords hit each other. They play for a long time. "I am getting hungry," says Tommy. "Let's go get our lunches out of our backpack," says Tammy Tough. Off they go.

Tommy opens up his backpack and pulls out his red lunch kit. Tammy Tough opens up her purple glitter backpack and pulls out her red glitter lunch kit. Tammy Tough even has a new blanket to use. She takes it out of her backpack. She and Tommy can sit on it. The kids enjoy eating their lunch together.

All of a sudden, two big kids climb up the ladder. The biggest kid yells, "Hey, get off ..." this fort because we want to play here by ourselves!" Tammy stands up and yells back, "No! We were here first, and we aren't leaving. Our Dad is a police officer and he's at the park right now. You have to leave!"

Tammy starts to call her Dad on her watch phone.
The boys look at each other and leave quickly.
Tammy saves the day!

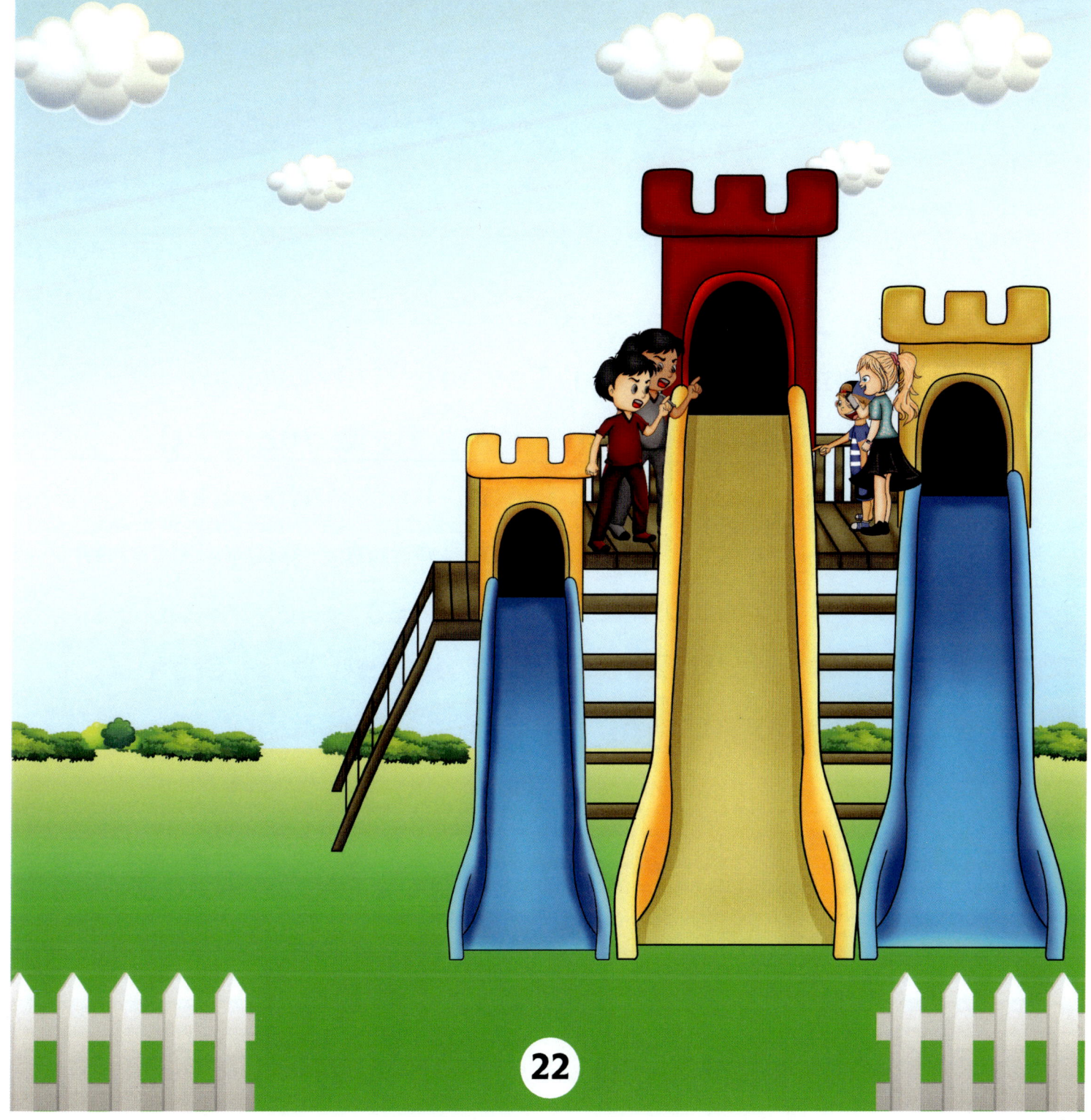

Tammy Tough and Tommy finish their lunches. Then, they pack up their lunch kit, fold the blanket, and put them into their backpack. Tammy Tough and Tommy play pirates a little longer on the fort. Then, they want to be near their Dad. He is by the basketball courts watching the teenagers play.

Tammy Tough and Tommy tell their Dad what happened with the two mean big boys. Their Dad said he was watching them while the big boys were up there. He saw the big boys leave. They finally decide to go home with their Dad. They tell their Mom about the fun adventures and how Tammy saved the day at the city park from the two mean big boys.

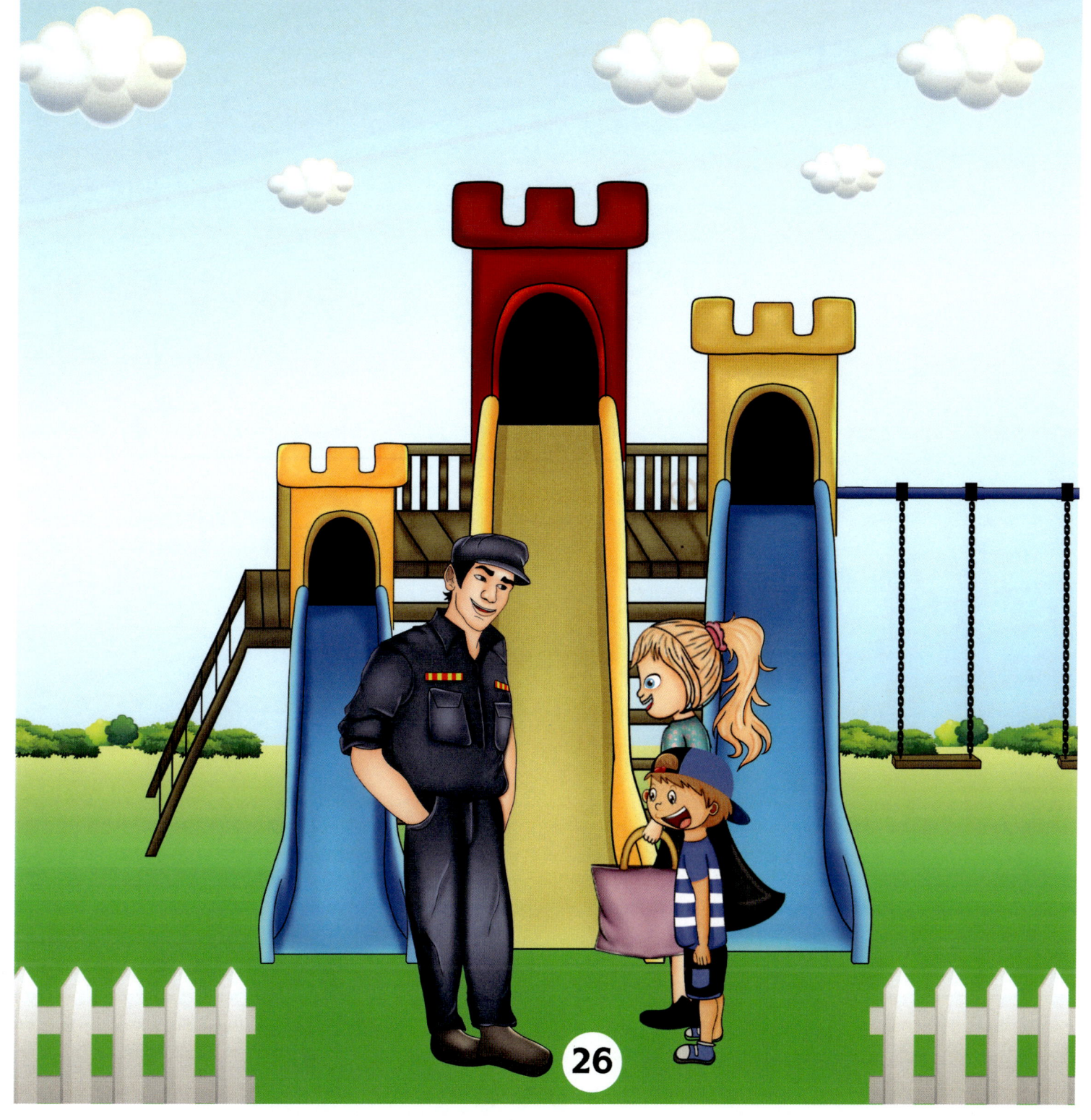

Made in the USA
Coppell, TX
20 July 2024